The Adventures of Paddington™

The Pet Show

HarperCollins *Children's Books*

Dear Aunt Lucy,

Today I learned that you can have a hidden talent. Any of us could be really good at something we've never tried before . . .

Paddington was walking in the park one day when he came across something rather exciting.

"What's going on, Ms Potts?" asked Paddington.

"It's the Windsor Gardens annual pet show," said Ms Potts.

Paddington didn't know what a pet show was.

"Everyone brings their pets to show off their talents," explained Ms Potts. "The whole thing's a hoot!"

Just then, Baaz, Simi and Judy arrived with their pets, followed by Mr Curry.

Cluck! Cluck! Oink! Oink! Squeak!

When Mr Curry discovered he could win a prize, he wanted to take part too and rushed off to find a pet . . .

"I'm entering . . . this cat," he said, holding up a stray cat that had just wandered by.

MEOWWWW!

"I don't know why any of you bothered," said Jonathan, arriving with his football. "Bally is going to win this thing hands down!"

"But Bally *isn't* an animal," said Judy.

"He is a *pet* and it is a *pet show*," said Jonathan.

"You're right," agreed Paddington. "It *is* a pet show . . ."

"Not any more," announced Ms Potts. "The pet show is cancelled."

Gasp!

"I forgot to tell the judge to come," explained Ms Potts. "And no judge means no show."

Everyone looked disappointed. They'd spent weeks teaching their pets routines and designing costumes.

"Paddington could be the judge," suggested Jonathan. "And then the show wouldn't need to be cancelled!"

Paddington wasn't sure but Ms Potts persuaded him. Everyone cheered – the pet show was on again!

"Welcome to the 532nd Windsor Gardens annual pet show!" Paddington declared, getting into the role. "Let's begin with the talent round. Good luck, everyone!"

First up was Baaz and his hens. He did a little dance while they clucked
away beautifully.

Bwwuck, buck,
bwwuck, buck, buck!

Clap, clap, clap!

"That was sensational, Baaz!" cheered Paddington. "You win!"

Ms Potts came running over. "No, no, no," she said. "You have to wait until you've seen the other acts, Paddington."

"Ah," said Paddington. "Of course."

Everyone performed in the talent round and Paddington watched, amazed.

Judy's gerbil jumped on to her head.

Squeak! Squeak!

Mr Gruber and Pigeonton performed a marvellous magic trick.

Coo! Coo!

Jonathan showed off
his skills with Bally.

Kick!

Bounce!

Kick!

And Lucky leaped
through Mateo's hoop.

Whoosh!

Woof! Woof!

"It's going to be **very** hard to choose who wins," said Paddington. "They're *all* so good!"

"Don't worry," said Ms Potts. "There are plenty of rounds left."

It was time for round two – the fashion round!

Ms Potts announced each of the contestants in turn as they appeared on the catwalk:

"Here is Lenny the gerbil, sporting a charming ruffle collar and pom-pom beret!"

"And here comes none other than the starlets of City Farm –
Heera and her hens!"

Cluck! Cluck! Cluck!

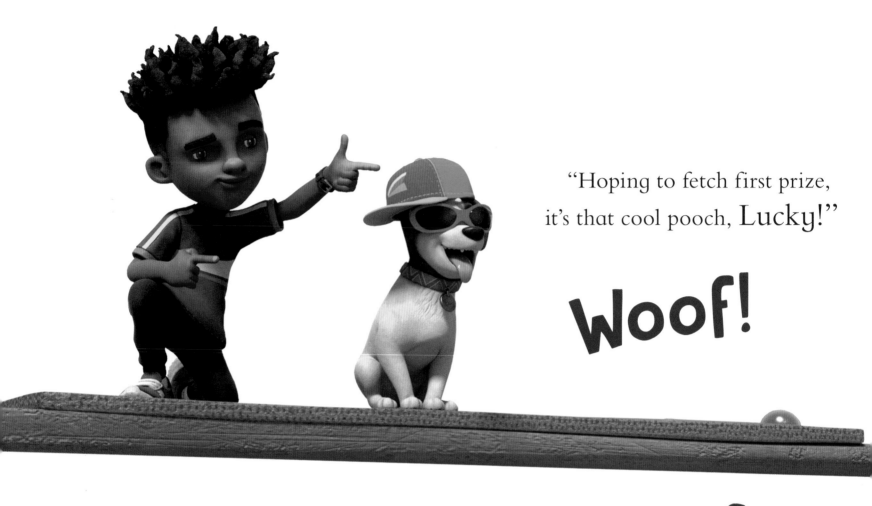

"Hoping to fetch first prize,
it's that cool pooch, Lucky!"

Woof!

"Well, howdy there, Sheriff Pigeonton!"
said Ms Potts.

After the fashion round finished, Paddington still couldn't decide which pet should win. They were all good. But if he didn't pick a winner, that would be unfair too. Everyone had worked so hard.

"Now for **the final round**," announced Ms Potts. "Each animal must complete **the obstacle course** as quickly as they can."

"It doesn't matter who's fastest," said Paddington. "I still want to be **friends** with **all** of you."

Woof!

The pets all tried their best, but the obstacle course was tricky. Some of the animals got a *little* confused about which way to go . . .

Miaow!

But Simi's pig, Erin, whizzed around in a super-fast time, hot on the heels of a carrot treat! Everyone cheered.

"Woohoo!"

It was time to announce who had won, but how was Paddington to decide?

"They all did **wonderful** things," Paddington told Ms Potts. "I can't pick a winner."

Then he had an idea . . .

He gave *each* of the competitors a slice of the prize cake and told them they were **all winners!** Everyone was delighted!

Sometimes you can be good at one thing and bad at another, Aunt Lucy. We all have our talents and strengths. I'm not very good at judging, but I think I might be good at making people happy!

Love from,

Paddington

We hope you enjoy this book.
Please return or renew it by the due date.
You can renew it at **www.norfolk.gov.uk/libraries**
or by using our free library app. Otherwise you can
phone **0344 800 8020** - please have your library
card and pin ready.
You can sign up for email reminders too.

7/22

NORFOLK COUNTY COUNCIL
LIBRARY AND INFORMATION SERVICE

NORFOLK ITEM

3 0129 08713 2107

For Bella
R.C.

For Noah and Zack
L.S.

LADYBIRD BOOKS

UK | USA | Canada | Ireland | Australia
India | New Zealand | South Africa

Ladybird Books is part of the Penguin Random House group of companies
whose addresses can be found at global.penguinrandomhouse.com.
www.penguin.co.uk   www.puffin.co.uk   www.ladybird.co.uk

Penguin
Random House
UK

First published 2022
001
Written by Rose Cobden. Text copyright © Ladybird Books Ltd, 2022
Illustrations copyright © Loretta Schauer, 2022
Printed in Italy

The authorized representative in the EEA is Penguin Random House Ireland,
Morrison Chambers, 32 Nassau Street, Dublin D02 YH68

A CIP catalogue record for this book is available from the British Library

ISBN: 978-0-241-55912-3
All correspondence to:
Ladybird Books
Penguin Random House Children's, One Embassy Gardens
8 Viaduct Gardens, London SW11 7BW

MIX
Paper from
responsible sources
FSC
www.fsc.org   FSC® C018179